aPE ESCaPE

WRITTEN BY
TRACEY WEST

ILLUSTRATED BY
JAMES ELSTON

Scholastic Inc.

New York · Toronto · London · Auckland · Sydney
Mexico City · New Delhi · Hong Kong · Buenos Aires

BAYO

ISBN-13: 978-0-545-07695-1
ISBN-10: 0-545-07695-1

Design by Aruna Goldstein

12 11 10 9 8 7 6 5 4 3 2 1   8 9 10 11 12 13/0

Printed in the U.S.A.

First Scholastic printing, April 2008

CHAPTER 1
PROMISES

Daniel Simmons stood in front of his third-grade class. He was nervous. He wasn't used to everyone watching him. *Mom has to talk in front of the camera all the time on her show,* he thought. *She never looks nervous. Maybe that means that I'll be good at it, too.*

"My oral report is about my trip to Australia," Daniel began. "My mom and dad went there to film an episode of *Pet Vet.*"

The whole class knew that Daniel's mom, Stacey Simmons, was the star of the *Pet Vet* show on the Critter Channel. In fact, every kid in Andrews Elementary School seemed to know that. People asked questions about his mom once in while. But most of time, Daniel was like everybody else. He liked it that way.

Daniel felt less nervous as his report went on. He talked about a koala mom and baby that were saved from a bushfire. Then he talked about Krissy, a koala that had broken her arm. She had a baby inside her pouch, but it hadn't come out yet.

"I was taking pictures of Krissy," Daniel said. "And then a little head popped out of her pouch. It was her joey—that's what a baby koala's called."

Daniel held up a picture he had taken of Krissy and her joey. He was relieved. The report was over!

"Very good, Daniel," said his teacher, Ms. Garcia. "Does anyone have any questions?"

Lots of hands went up in the air. Ms. Garcia called on a girl named Cassie in the front row.

"How many wild animals have you seen up close?" she asked.

Daniel had to think for a minute. He got to travel with his mom a lot. He had seen all kinds of wild animals. "I'm not sure," Daniel answered. "There were koala bears in Australia. And I've been up close to a lion, and a dolphin, and penguins, and—"

The class all began to talk at once. They called out their questions at the same time.

"Penguins? I love penguins! They're so cute!"

"Did you swim with the dolphin?"

"You mean you got to be in the same room with a lion?"

Ms. Garcia held up two fingers. That was the signal for everyone to be quiet. Everyone stopped talking. "Please raise your hand if you have a question," she reminded the class.

A boy named David raised his hand first. "Can you bring a wild animal into class?"

The class got noisy again. Everyone wanted to see a wild animal up close!

Daniel was surprised. "Uh— I don't know," he stammered.

"Your mom's the Pet Vet!" a girl added in.

"You've probably got lots of cool animals at your house…you could bring one of them in!"

Daniel frowned. "Not exactly," he began. They always went to zoos or centers to see wild animals. The only animals that his mom had were at the animal hospital, and those belonged to their owners.

Then Miranda raised her hand. She lived down the street from Daniel. "My mom knows the star of the TV show *Eddie's World*," she said. "I bet I can get Eddie to come into class and meet everyone."

That got the class excited again. *Eddie's World* was the number one show on the KidPlanet Channel. The show starred a ten-year-old whiz kid named Eddie Morales. He played guitar in his own rock band and did skateboard tricks. Everybody in third grade watched *Eddie's World* every Friday night.

Daniel was annoyed. He knew Miranda was just trying to show off. "I'll bring an animal to class!" he blurted out. "A really good one!"

Ms. Garcia stood up and the class quieted down. "Thank you, Daniel and Miranda," she said. "But you shouldn't promise anything without asking permission first."

The lunch bell rang. Daniel put his koala pictures in his desk and got in line next to his best friend, Abigail Ahn.

"Are you really going to bring a wild animal to class?" Abigail whispered.

"Um, I don't know." Daniel answered. "I guess I just said that since Miranda said all that stuff about Eddie. She always tries to be better than everybody else."

Abigail shook her head. "I don't think your mom's going to let you."

"Maybe she will—I'll ask her," Daniel replied. But deep inside, Daniel knew Abigail was right. He frowned. *I'll figure something out,* he thought. *Or everyone will think I'm a liar!*

CHAPTER 2
CHIMP EMERGENCY!

"Today *Pet Vet* is here at Joyful Jungle," Stacey said. She smiled into the camera. "It's a sanctuary for chimpanzees here in California. I'm here with Sabrina Michaels, the director of Joyful Jungle."

Sabrina was a short woman who smiled a lot. She wore her dark hair in braids. A chimpanzee was on her back. The ape had brown fur

and its long arms were wrapped around her neck. The chimp looked very comfortable.

"All of the chimps here were rescued," Sabrina explained. "They were taken from their homes in Africa to be pets or to be on TV. But when they got older, their owners didn't want them anymore."

Daniel stood behind the camera and watched his mom film the show. It was Saturday, so he didn't have school. His dad, Will, was working the camera. Ron, the director, sat in a chair and watched the action. His little dog Peanut sat in a tiny director's chair next to him.

Daniel thought Joyful Jungle was a great place. The chimps lived in a big area outside. Lots of trees and plants grew there. When they drove up, Daniel could see chimps sitting in the branches and munching on food. Now they were filming in an exam room inside the building.

Stacey reached out her arms to the chimp on Sabrina's back. The chimp climbed into her arms. "This is Marcus," Stacey said. "He's a male common chimpanzee. Marcus is eight years old and weighs about seventy-five pounds."

"Marcus was born in Central Africa," Sabrina chimed in. "He was taken from his home when he was just a little baby. Joyful Jungle isn't exactly like the home Marcus left, but we try to make it as close as we can."

Stacey placed Marcus on the exam table. "Marcus is a healthy chimp. Today he's going to help show us what a chimp needs to eat to stay healthy."

Sabrina placed a bowl on the table. It had pieces of fruit in it. It also had what looked like a bunch of big meatballs. Marcus quickly grabbed an apple slice and bit into it. He looked very happy.

"In the wild, chimps eat a diet of fruits, leaves, plants, and insects," Stacey explained. "It's important that they eat lots of good food when they're in captivity. Otherwise, they can stop growing or get sick."

Sabrina picked up one of the balls in the bowl. "This is a treat we make. It's made of rice and beans, which are good for our chimps. It also has palm oil, which keeps the chimps' fur and skin healthy."

Marcus spotted the ball in Sabrina's hands. He dropped the apple slice and grabbed the ball instead. Then he chomped into it.

Suddenly, Peanut gave a little yip. He ran over to the exam table.

"Peanut!" Ron hissed. He was trying to be quiet so they wouldn't ruin the segment. "Get back here! You're not supposed to be on TV! Bad dog!"

Peanut stood on his hind legs. He began to

whine. He was staring at the treat in Marcus's hand. Everyone started to laugh.

"Cut!" Ron yelled.

Marcus stopped chewing and cocked his head. He looked at Peanut. Then he took another ball from the bowl and got off the exam table. Marcus tossed the treat to Peanut, who caught it in his mouth. Peanut chewed the treat noisily as he ran back to his little chair.

Ron stood up, shaking his head. "Bad Peanut! Now we have to do it again."

"Maybe you could leave it in," Daniel suggested. "That was pretty funny."

Sabrina smiled. "I've never seen Marcus share food before. He must really like Peanut."

Just then, a man ran into the room. He wore a Joyful Jungle shirt. "We've got an emergency!" he cried. "A chimp is hurt!"

CHAPTER 3
BAYO'S ESCAPE

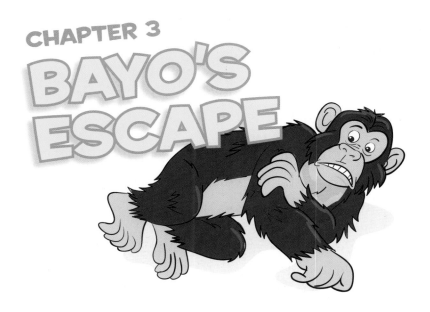

Everyone ran outside. Will brought along the TV camera. They all stopped at the outdoor chimp area. A small chimp was lying on the ground, next to the fence.

"Bayo tried to get out again," the man explained. "She made a hole high up in the fence and fell as she was trying to climb out."

Sabrina and Stacey knelt down. They both checked out Bayo.

"She's awake," Stacey said. "I don't think she

hit her head. But her arm might need help. We should take her to the exam room."

Sabrina and the worker gently picked up Bayo. They carried her back to the exam room. Everyone followed.

Will filmed as Bayo was placed on the exam table. Stacey looked at the camera.

"A chimpanzee can get very upset when it's hurt," she said. "We'll give Bayo something to make her sleep while we look at her arm and treat her."

Stacey gave Bayo a shot. The chimp's eyes closed. Then Stacey gently touched her arm. "I think it's just a sprain," she said, "but we'll need an X-ray to be sure."

While Bayo was in the X-ray room, Ron set Sabrina up in front of the camera to talk about Bayo. "Bayo is four years old," Sabrina explained. "She hasn't been in Joyful Jungle very long. She's tried to escape a lot already. The other chimps keep busy by grooming each other and building nests in the trees. But Bayo isn't interested—she seems bored."

Bayo's X-rays were done. Will filmed Stacey as she checked them.

"No broken bones," Stacey said. "Just a sprain. I'll put Bayo's arm in a sling until it gets better." Stacey slid Bayo's arm into the sling and strapped it across Bayo's chest. "The sling will keep the arm straight so it can heal quickly," she explained.

Bayo began to wake up. She slowly opened her eyes and looked up at Stacey.

"We'll keep Bayo indoors tonight," Sabrina said. "Then we'll make sure she doesn't try to escape again."

"Bayo should be feeling better soon," Stacey said. "We'll check up with her again in a few weeks. Stay tuned for more *Pet Vet!*"

"Cut!" Ron cried.

Sabrina took Bayo to another room while the crew packed up the equipment. Daniel walked up to his mom.

"Poor Bayo," he said. "I hope she'll be all right."

Stacey ruffled Daniel's brown hair. "I'm sure she'll be fine, honey," she said. "I'm going to check on her before we leave. Want to come with me?"

"Yes!" Daniel said.

Daniel helped the crew clean up. Then he and his mom went to see Bayo. She was in a big cage in a room all by herself. Bayo was facing the wall. Sabrina sat on a chair next to her.

"I hate leaving her in a cage," Sabrina said. "But we have to make sure she doesn't get hurt again. Her arm needs to get better first."

Daniel walked up to the cage. "Hello, Bayo," he said quietly. "I'm Daniel."

Bayo slowly turned around. She looked into Daniel's eyes. Daniel thought her brown eyes were very pretty.

"You'll be out of here soon," he told her.

Bayo walked over to Daniel. She held out her good arm. Her small fingers reached through the bars.

"Can I touch her?" Daniel asked.

"You can touch her hand," Sabrina told him. "Be gentle."

Daniel held out his hand. Bayo wrapped her fingers around it.

Sabrina stood up. "Hey," she said, "I think you've made a friend, Daniel. Bayo hasn't warmed up to any of us here at Joyful Jungle like this."

"Daniel's very good with animals." Stacey smiled proudly.

"I'd love it if Daniel could come back," Sabrina said. "I think a visit would be good for Bayo."

Daniel looked at the chimp's sweet face. *Bayo likes me!* It made him feel special.

"That sounds awesome," he said.

CHAPTER 4
MONKEY BUSINESS

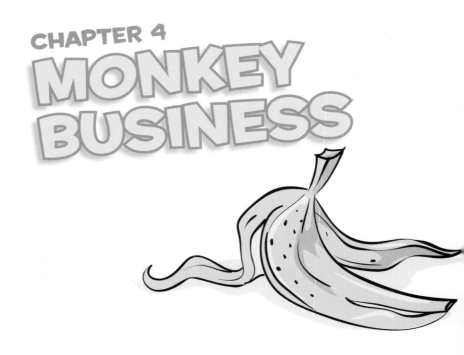

Daniel told Abigail about Bayo on Monday at recess. "She was trying to escape," he explained. "I guess she doesn't like it at Joyful Jungle. It's a really great place. I hope she gets used to it."

"You're so lucky." Abigail sighed. "I wish I could be friends with a chimpanzee."

"Wow, you're really friends with a monkey?"

Daniel and Abigail turned to see David

standing next to them. "Actually, she's a chimp," Daniel replied. "Her name's Bayo."

"Cool!" David said. "That's the animal you're bringing to class, right?"

Suddenly Cassie showed up, too. "What's Daniel bringing to class?" she asked.

"A chimpanzee," David replied. "It'll be awesome!"

"Um, I don't think—" Daniel began.

But it was too late. Cassie was already yelling to everyone in the school yard. "Daniel's getting a chimpanzee for us!"

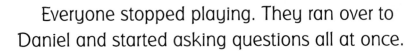

Everyone stopped playing. They ran over to Daniel and started asking questions all at once.

"Can we hold the chimpanzee?"

"When are you bringing it in?"

"Do chimps like bananas?"

"But—um." Daniel hesitated. *I don't want to look like a liar,* he thought. "We'll see," he finally said.

After everyone was gone, Abigail turned to Daniel. "Did your mom say that you could bring in a chimp?" she asked.

Daniel didn't say anything. Abigail shook her head. "Then you shouldn't have said that, Daniel."

"I know," Daniel said sadly. "I'll talk to my

mom today. Maybe she can ask if I can bring
Bayo here."

"Definitely not," Stacey said. Daniel and
Stacey were in the *Pet Vet* van. They were driving
to Joyful Jungle for a visit. "A wild animal belongs
in the wild," she added. "Or in a safe place, like
Joyful Jungle."

Daniel knew his mom would say no, but he
still felt disappointed. "I know," he said. "I just—
sort of—promised my friends that I'd bring a real
wild animal to class."

"I'm sure we could bring in a nice cat or a dog,"
Stacey said. "Ron would love to show off Peanut.

Or maybe Pirate Bill would bring in Jolly Roger."

Daniel knew that Peanut was a very cute dog. And Jolly Roger, the parrot, could talk. But they wouldn't be the same. His friends were expecting a chimpanzee. "Never mind," Daniel said, looking out the window.

Stacey parked the van in front of Joyful Jungle. They stepped out into the sunshine. Daniel held a bunch of bananas. They were a present for Bayo. Then Stacey clipped something onto Daniel's shirt.

"What's this?" Daniel asked.

"It's an official *Pet Vet* name tag," Stacey said. "Ron got them. Now when we go places, people will know we're with the show."

NAME
DANIEL SIMMONS

Daniel looked down at the name tag. It had the *Pet Vet* logo on it. His name was on it in capital letters: DANIEL SIMMONS.

"Neat," Daniel said.

"Sabrina told me that Bayo is still indoors," Stacey explained. "We'll go visit her there." They walked past the outdoor chimp area. A few curious chimps came up to the fence to greet them. Daniel stopped. "Hi, guys," he said.

Suddenly, one of the chimps reached through the fence. The chimp yanked the bananas out of Daniel's hand. "Hey!" Daniel cried. "I need those! They're for Bayo!"

The chimp pulled one banana off the bunch. The rest of the bunch fell to the ground. Before Daniel could pick them up, more chimps ran over and grabbed the rest of the bananas behind the fence! "Give it back!" Daniel cried.

The first chimp stopped. He held out a banana. Daniel reached out to grab it. In a flash, the chimp pulled it back. Daniel frowned. "No fair!"

Stacey laughed behind him. "I think he's playing a game with you."

Daniel put his hands on his hips. "Please?" he asked the chimp. "I really need that banana."

The chimp looked at the banana. He looked at Daniel. He held out the banana. Daniel reached for it. The chimp pulled the banana away again! He began to make a noise that sounded like a laugh: *Ook ook ook!*

"That's not funny!" Daniel cried.

Then another chimp walked up. "That looks like Marcus," Stacey said.

Marcus grabbed the banana from the chimp. The chimp stopped laughing. Marcus handed the banana through the fence and Daniel took it.

"Thanks, Marcus," Daniel said.

Ook! Marcus replied.

"At least I have one banana for Bayo," Daniel said. "We'd better go in before I lose it again."

They found Sabrina inside, next to Bayo's cage. There were three padlocks on the cage door. Stacey raised an eyebrow when she saw the locks.

"She's escaped the cage twice already,"

Sabrina said, shaking her head. "I'm sorry she wants to run away. But she's got to understand that this is the best place for her."

"I'm sure she'll figure that out soon," Stacey said.

Bayo was curled up in a corner of the cage. When she saw Daniel, she walked over to him.

Daniel held out the banana. "For you, Bayo," he said.

Bayo took the banana. Then she grabbed Daniel's fingers. She shook them up and down.

"Mom, I think she's saying thank you!" Daniel said.

Daniel talked to Bayo for a while. He told her about the banana-stealing chimp. "Marcus helped me get it back. You'll like Marcus," he promised.

"She'll meet Marcus soon," Stacey said. "I'm

going to remove the sling on Saturday. Then she can go back outside."

"It's fun outside, Bayo," Daniel told the chimp. "You'll like it there. I promise."

But Daniel felt bad after he said the words. He'd made another promise he wasn't sure he could keep. *What if Bayo doesn't like it outside? What if she tries to escape again?*

CHAPTER 5

BANANA YELLOW

For the rest of the week, everyone at school asked Daniel the same question:

"When are you bringing the chimpanzee?"

"Uh, soon," Daniel would say. He knew he should tell the truth. But he didn't want everyone to be mad.

On Friday, Miranda said, "I bet Daniel isn't going to bring in a chimpanzee at all."

"Yeah? Well, I bet you're not going to bring in Eddie from *Eddie's World*, either," Daniel replied.

Miranda blushed. She didn't say anything about the chimpanzee again.

That didn't make Daniel feel much better. He knew if he didn't bring a chimp into class soon, everyone would know he'd been lying.

"You should just tell the truth now," Abigail told him.

"I know," Daniel said. "But maybe Mom will change her mind. I'm going to ask one more time."

The next Saturday, Abigail came with Daniel to Joyful Jungle. Ron gave Abigail her very own name tag. The TV crew set up in the exam room.

Stacey stood by the exam table. She smiled at the camera. "We're back at Joyful Jungle to check on Bayo, the chimp who sprained her arm," Stacey said. "Today, I'm going to take off Bayo's sling. Then she can go back outside with the other chimps."

Sabrina brought Bayo into the exam room. It didn't take long for Stacey to take off the sling. Bayo sat patiently. Stacey gently moved the chimp's arm up and down.

"Good as new!" Stacey said.

"We'll put Bayo in a space by herself outside at first," Sabrina said. "Then, when she gets comfortable, we'll move her in with the other chimps." Sabrina looked over at Daniel and grinned. "We might bring in a special friend to keep her company, though."

"Cut!" Ron yelled. "Great segment!"

Daniel was excited. He ran up to Sabrina. "Can I really stay with Bayo?" he asked.

Sabrina nodded. "I'd like to try it for a while. I think it'll cheer her up."

"Can Abigail come, too?" Daniel asked.

"Sure," Sabrina said. "I'll be there to make sure everything is OK."

Sabrina brought Bayo outside. They went to a small, fenced-in area. It was attached to the main chimp habitat, but a fence separated the two parts. Sabrina set Bayo down on the grass. She brought out a blanket for Daniel and Abigail and sat down on the blanket with them.

Bayo came right over and sat down next to Daniel. She looked up at him.

"Hi, Bayo," Daniel said. Then he had an idea. He had his camera with him. "Can I take your picture?"

Ook! Bayo hooted. It was the first time Daniel had heard her voice.

Daniel aimed the camera. He got a great close-up of Bayo's face. He looked at the picture on the camera's tiny screen. "Look," he said, showing Abigail.

"Ooh, that's nice!" she said. "I wish I had a camera—wait!"

Abigail took her purple backpack off of her back. "I can draw a picture of Bayo!"

She took out a notebook with glittery stars on the cover and a small box of crayons. "Let me see," she said. She dumped the crayons onto the blanket. "I need a nice peach...."

Abigail began to draw Bayo's face on the page. She used black to draw Bayo's eyes and mouth. Then she used brown to draw Bayo's fur. Bayo slowly inched toward Abigail. She watched as Abigail drew.

Abigail held up the finished drawing. "What do

you think, Bayo?" she asked. "Do you like it?"

Ook! Bayo replied. She looked excited. She reached over and grabbed a yellow crayon from the pile. Then she waved her arm up and down.

Daniel couldn't believe it. "I think she wants to draw something," he said.

"OK, Bayo," Abigail said. She turned to a blank page in the notebook and slid it over. "Draw here." She pointed to the paper.

Bayo gripped the crayon in her hand. She made big yellow swirls all over the paper. "That looks nice, Bayo," Daniel said.

Bayo handed the crayon to Daniel. Then she picked up an orange crayon. She drew more swirls on the paper.

"Look at her go!" Daniel said. He passed the crayon back to Abigail. As he did, he noticed something. "Hey, look!" he said. "Bayo picked the banana yellow crayon!"

Abigail looked at the crayon and laughed. "I guess she knows what she likes."

Sabrina watched them, looking interested. "Hmmm, Bayo really seems to like drawing.

I wonder...."

Bayo threw down the orange crayon. She picked up the notebook. Then she waved it at Daniel. "All done?" Daniel asked. He took the notebook from her. Then he tore the drawing out of the notebook. "Can I keep it, Bayo?"

Ook! Bayo replied.

Abigail leaned over. "That's nice! I wish I had a drawing like that."

Bayo grabbed the notebook back. She picked up a blue crayon. Then she began to color on the page.

Stacey came into the fenced-in area. "It looks like Bayo's having fun," she said. "You and Abigail are really good with animals."

"Thanks, Mom," Daniel said. But he was frowning.

"What's wrong?" Stacey asked.

Daniel sighed. "I never told the kids at school that I couldn't bring Bayo to class. They still think she's coming. I was going to ask you again if I could bring her, but I know that's not right. I'm going to have to tell the truth, like Abigail said."

"Telling the truth is a good idea," Stacey said. She glanced over at Sabrina. "You know, we definitely can't bring Bayo to class. But maybe there's something else we can do...."

CHAPTER 6

THE BEST TRIP EVER

"Welcome to *Pet Vet*," Stacey said. "We're back at Joyful Jungle with an update on our favorite chimp, Bayo. And today we have some special guests with us. Let's give a special welcome to Ms. Garcia's class from Andrews Elementary!"

Will turned the camera away from Stacey. Daniel and his classmates stood with their teacher, Ms. Garcia. They all waved to the camera.

Stacey had helped Daniel keep the promise he had made — sort of. Instead of bringing a chimp to class, they brought the class to the chimp! The class watched quietly as Stacey filmed the show.

"Three weeks ago, Bayo's sling was removed," Stacey said. "She hurt her arm trying to escape. Sabrina, the director of Joyful Jungle, told us that Bayo was bored. But Bayo isn't bored anymore."

Stacey pointed inside the chimp area. The chimpanzees were doing what they normally did. Some were building nests in the trees. Others were grooming each other. Others were eating.

Bayo wasn't doing any of that. She was sitting at a small table under a tree. Sabrina stood behind her. There were paper and crayons on the table. Bayo was busy drawing a picture.

"Bayo likes to draw," Stacey explained. "She draws every day. Making pictures seems to keep her happy. And she hasn't tried to escape once."

Bayo finished her picture and held it up. It was a pretty design of orange and yellow swirls. Marcus the chimp walked up to the table. Bayo handed the picture to him.

Ook! Marcus said. He took the picture and looked at it.

"Bayo has a new friend, too," Stacey explained. "She likes to draw pictures for her friend Marcus."

Daniel felt good that Bayo had a new friend. Marcus was a very nice chimp. Daniel still wanted to be her friend, and visit as much as he could. But it was good for Bayo to have other friends, too.

"Cut!" Ron yelled. "This is fantastic! A chimp that draws! Kids! A happy ending! What could be better? This is going to be great TV!"

Yip! Yip! agreed Peanut.

Ms. Garcia smiled at the class. "This was a wonderful class trip. We need to thank Dr. Simmons for arranging things for us."

"Thanks, Dr. Simmons!" everyone said at once.

Stacey walked up and put her arm around Daniel. "I'm glad you could all come," she said. "And in a few weeks, you'll see your class trip on TV!" Everyone cheered.

Daniel tugged on his mom's sleeve. "Thanks, Mom," he said. "You really helped me out."

"You're welcome," she said. "And I'd like to thank you and Abigail, too. You really helped out Bayo."

Daniel's classmates gathered around him. "This is the best field trip ever," David said.

"It's even better than having a chimp in the classroom," Cassie said. "Now we get to see lots of chimps."

"Well, wild animals belong in the wild," Daniel said, looking up at his mom. Stacey winked at him. "I'm going to say good-bye to Bayo," Daniel said. He walked over to the fence.

Bayo ran over when she saw Daniel. She had a picture in her hand.

"Another picture for me, Bayo? Daniel asked. He pulled the paper through one of the spaces in the fence. He unrolled it. "Hey, look at this!" he cried.

Abigail ran up to him. "What is it?"

Daniel held up the picture. Bayo had drawn something yellow. Something long. It wasn't just a bunch of swirls. It looked perfect.

"It's a banana!" Daniel cried. "Bayo, you're amazing!"

Bayo seemed to smile. *Ook!*

STOP MONKEYING AROUND!

Log on to **www.scholastic.com/petvet** for a brand-new *Pet Vet Club* website episode! Download fun crafts and puzzles, treat a virtual chimpanzee, and send a friend a *Pet Vet Club* e-card.

This month's password is:

BANANA

Turn to page 48 of your *Pet Vet Club* chapter book every month for a new password to unlock a new level of the *Pet Vet Club* website. See you online!